Catching the Wild Waiyuuzee

Rita Williams-Garcia

illustrated by
Mike Reed

Simon & Schuster Books for Young Readers

NEW YORK   LONDON   TORONTO   SYDNEY   SINGAPORE

SIMON & SCHUSTER BOOKS FOR YOUNG READERS An imprint of
Simon & Schuster Children's Publishing Division, 1230 Avenue of the Americas,
New York, New York 10020. Text copyright © 2000 by Rita Williams-Garcia.
Illustrations copyright © 2000 by Mike Reed. All rights reserved including the right
of reproduction in whole or in part in any form. SIMON & SCHUSTER BOOKS FOR YOUNG
READERS is a trademark of Simon & Schuster. Book design by Anahid Hamparian.
The text for this book is set in Geometric 706. The illustrations were rendered in
Photoshop. Printed in United States of America   10 9 8 7 6 5 4 3 2 1
LIBRARY OF CONGRESS CATALOGING-IN-PUBLICATION DATA: Williams-Garcia, Rita.
Catching the wild waiyuuzee / by Rita Williams-Garcia ; illustrated by Mike Reed.
p. cm. Summary: As she tries to escape her mother's efforts to "plait-a-plait" and
"string-a-bead" her hair, a young girl imagines herself running away into a jungle.
ISBN 0-689-82601-X [1. Hair—Fiction. 2. Mothers and daughters—Fiction.
3. Afro-Americans—Fiction.] I. Reed, Mike, 1951-   , ill. II. Title.
PZ7.W6713 Cat 2000   [E]—dc21   98-49497   CIP AC

first *edition*

To Stephanie Elaine,
my own Wild Waiyuuzee
—R. Wms.-G.

To Jane, Alex, and Joe
—M. R.

Out of
the bush ran
the Wild Waiyuuzee.

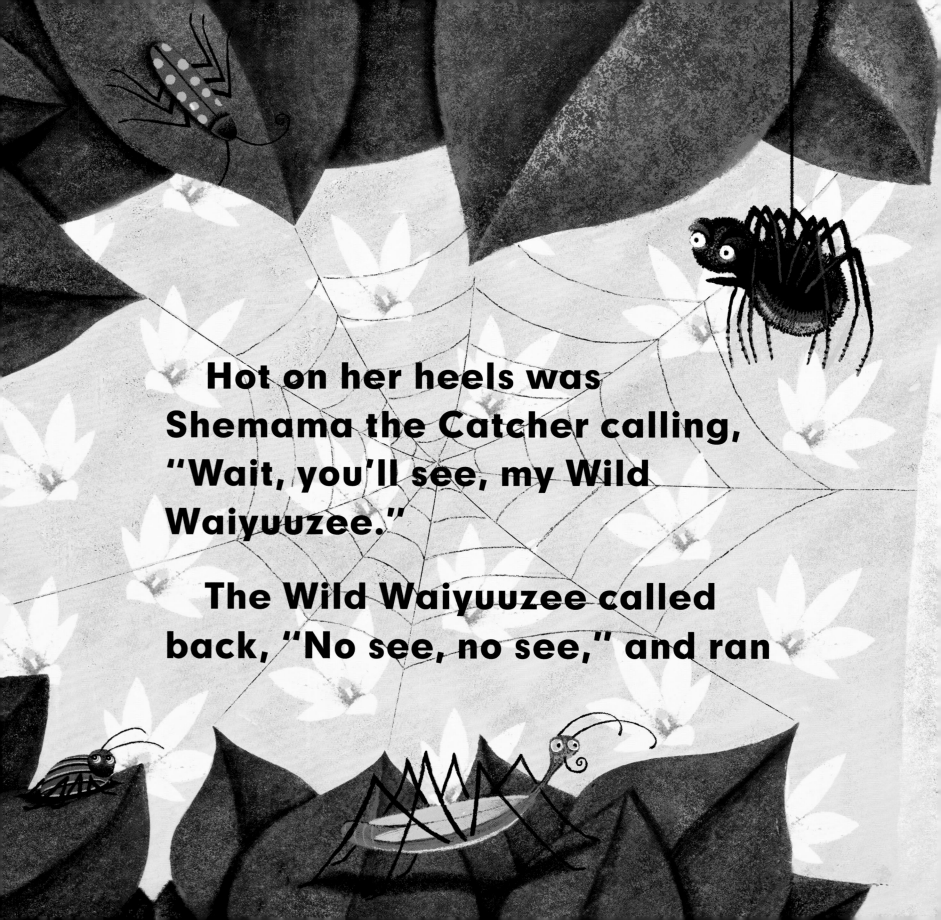

Hot on her heels was Shemama the Catcher calling, "Wait, you'll see, my Wild Waiyuuzee."

The Wild Waiyuuzee called back, "No see, no see," and ran

Tippi Tappi

Tappi Tappi

deep into the mango grove.

TRUMPI
TRUMPI

Shemama coming foot and foot after the Wild Waiyuuzee.

Oh, how the Wild Waiyuuzee wanted to wiggle and giggle as all Wild Waiyuuzees do.

But she stood still like rock,
hoping to trick Shemama.

Shemama called out,
"I'm going to spray you
with my jumbo sprayer!"

"Eee no! Eee no!" squealed
the Wild Waiyuuzee.

Splee-ZASH! went the water.

Wetty wet-wet!

The Wild Waiyuuzee rolled out of the high grass and into an iguana cave.

All was quiet. All was safe. Until . . .

BANG-O-BOK! BANG-O-BOK!

Shemama started cracking nut-nuts for nut-nut oil.

Ah, ko!
The very thing needed to catch a Wild Waiyuuzee.

"I'm going to oil you, my Wild Waiyuuzee."

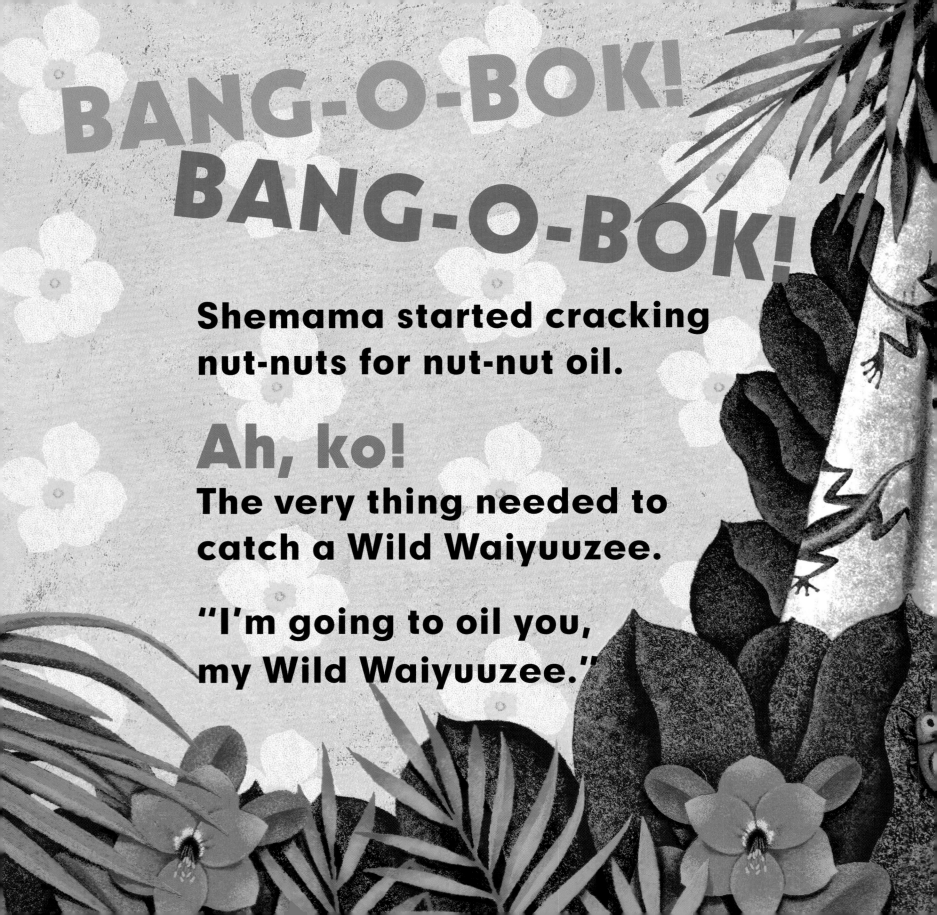

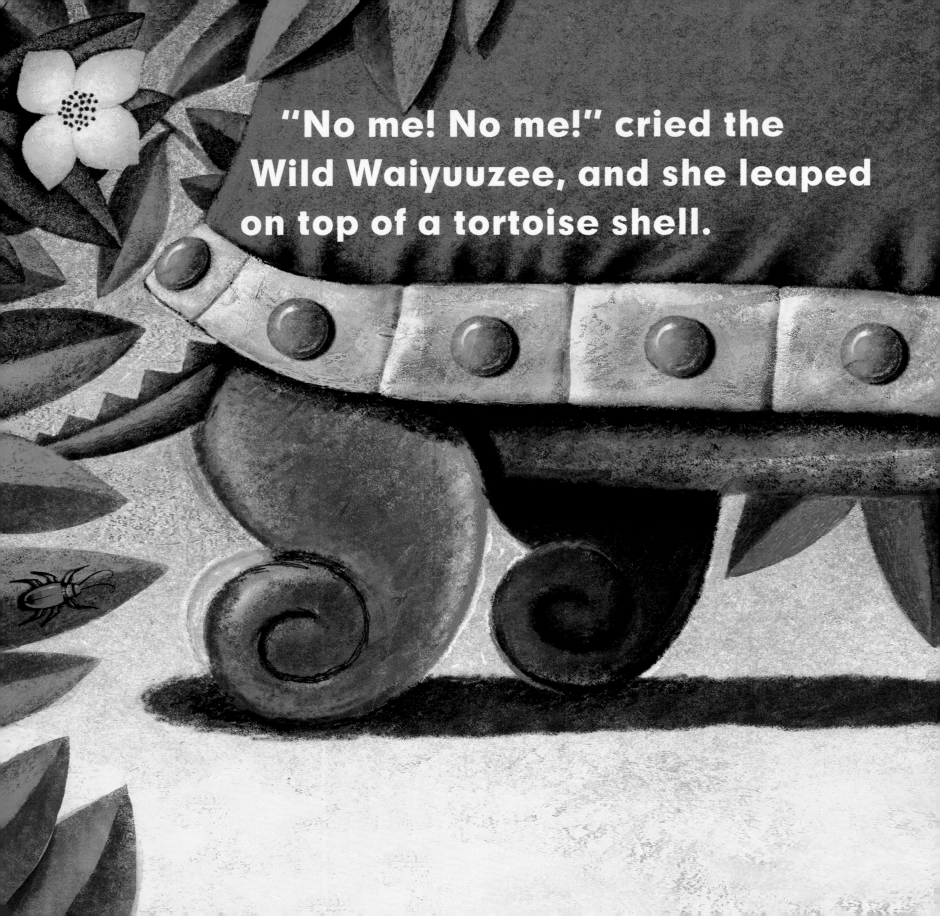

"No me! No me!" cried the Wild Waiyuuzee, and she leaped on top of a tortoise shell.

But tortoise moved slow as tortoise do. . . .

so Shemama caught that
Wild Waiyuuzee and

PATTI PATTI

RUB RUB

put nut-nut oil on that
nut-nut head.

But one good wiggle
and the Wild Waiyuuzee was free.

Off she ran

Tippi Tappi

Tippi Tappi

back into the bush.

Shemama hopping hot foot now. "I'm going to comb you with my piney pig's tail."

"Hee hee. No me," said the Wild Waiyuuzee.

"Then I'm going to plait-a-plait and string-a-bead. Wait, you'll see."

TRUMPI TRUMPI

**Shemama went foot and foot
into the bush after the Wild Waiyuuzee.**

TRUMP! TRUMP!

Oh, how the Wild Waiyuuzee
wanted to be still like a rock,
but shook top and bottom
when she heard . . .

But, ah, ko!
Nowhere to go.

"Come, come, little one" said Shemama.

"No owie owie me?" asked the Wild Waiyuuzee.

"No owie owie."

"Moka true?"

"Moka true."

The Wild Waiyuuzee
came wee foot and foot
out of the bush . . .

and into Shemama's arms.

With piney pig's tail, thumb, and fingers, Shemama made plait-a-plait and string-a-bead each one.

**Then they came
and stood before their look so selves.**

"You see!" Mama said.
"Hee hee. Me see," her little one said.

Ah, ko! Beautiful.
And she wiggled and giggled
as little girls do.